COOL CATS TAP

BOOK 2

by Josephine Page
Illustrated by Matt Straub

SCHOLASTIC INC.

Cartwheel
·B·O·O·K·S·®

New York   Toronto   London   Auckland   Sydney
Mexico City   New Delhi   Hong Kong   Buenos Aires

I am Matt.
I am a cool cat.

I tap.
Tap tap.

I am Tom.
I am a cool cat.

I tap the top
of a pot.
Tap tap.

I am Pat.
I am a cool cat.

I toot.
Toot toot.

I am Sam.
I am a cool cat.

I toot, too.
Toot toot toot.

Stop!
Stop the tap.
Stop the toot.

I am Pam.
I am a cop.

I tap, too!
Tap tap tap.

I am a cool cop!

Yes.